Richard Doyle, Charles Perrault, George Dalziel, Edward
Dalziel

An old fairy tale: The sleeping beauty

Richard Doyle, Charles Perrault, George Dalziel, Edward Dalziel

An old fairy tale: The sleeping beauty

ISBN/EAN: 9783337120887

Printed in Europe, USA, Canada, Australia, Japan

Cover: Foto ©Andreas Hilbeck / pixelio.de

More available books at **www.hansebooks.com**

AN OLD FAIRY TALE.

THE

SLEEPING BEAUTY.

BY

RICHARD DOYLE AND J. R. PLANCHE.

The Pictures Engraved by the Brothers Dalziel.

LONDON:

GEORGE ROUTLEDGE AND SONS,

THE BROADWAY, LUDGATE.

NEW YORK: 416 BROOME STREET.

1868.

PREFACE.

Mr. RICHARD DOYLE having made several designs from the popular Fairy Tale, " The Sleeping Beauty in the Wood," I was requested by the Messrs. DALZIEL to furnish them with a versification of the story to accompany the engravings. The lines in italics refer to the woodcuts, to describe which they have been expressly written; and this will account for any little variation in detail from the original version.

J. R. PLANCHÉ.

LONDON, *November*, 1865.

LIST OF ILLUSTRATIONS.

" A beauteous face with starry eyes,
And streaming hair, with blossoms wild
Crowned as a Fairy Queen should be."

AN OLD FAIRY TALE.

"ONCE on a time"—O words of power !—
    Recalling many a charméd hour,
When, nestled in some quiet nook,
Clutching the last new Fairy book,

The welcome gift of Granddame kind,
Or—which, perhaps, more pleasure brought—
" With my own money" proudly bought!
Over its magic leaves I leant,
     To all things else deaf, dumb, and blind,
In mingled awe and wonderment;
Devouring each adventure strange,
 Enchanted by each startling change,
Sharing the childless Queen's concern
     That still the stars should prove contrary,
As much surprised as she to learn
     The fish she rescued was a Fairy!
And when unwillingly to bed
From the bewitching volume led,
With slumber combating in vain,
What visions crowded on my brain
Of palaces with countless halls,
And golden gates, and jasper walls;
Gardens where all the flowers were gems,
Ruby roses with emerald stems;
Fountains that danced in the perfumed air,
And bright forms fluttering everywhere!

Then all would melt, and fuse, and fade,
As heavier down my eyelids weighed,
And in a misty moonlit glade,
A beauteous face with starry eyes,
 And streaming hair, with blossoms wild
 Crowned as a Fairy Queen should be,
  Peep through a world of leaves, and smile
 As might a mother on her child ;
And tiny Sprites in quaintest guise
   Up through the tangled branches climb,
 And leap and swing in elfin glee,
  And 'mid their gambols, all the while
Make merry mops and mows at me,—
    Once on a time !—Once on a time !

Once on a time !—Why, even now,
With seventy winters on my brow,
I feel the power of the spell,
And on the pleasant pages dwell
With all the fresh and dear delight
That made my boyhood's dream so bright !

4

Pages that rivalry defy !
Tales which, though centuries sweep by,
Are new as when they first were told,
And never, never can be old !
Like to the pure and glassy brooks
 Which have for generations been
Mirrors of childhood's joyous looks,
 Disporting on their margents green ;
And on from age to age still run
 Through the same wild and flow'ry ways,
Shining as brightly in the sun,
 And gladdening all who on them gaze !

But peace, thou garrulous old man,
 Well-nigh a child again, indeed !
Forbear these memories to scan,
 And briefly with thy task proceed ;—
The flattering task, to be a foil
To the fine pencil of a Doyle.

Once more, then—Once upon a time—
For be it or in prose or rhyme,

The Abode of the Wicked Fairy.

A Fairy tale should so begin—
A King and Queen
Enthroned were seen,
A lovely, loyal isle within.
Their crowns to wear
Without a care,
One blessing only they had wanted—
To that sea-girdled realm an heir;
And Fate at length their wish had granted.
It was a girl ; but quite contented
They gazed upon the little maid.
No odious Salique law prevented.
By her the sceptre being swayed;
And they had heard of an isle afar
Where a Queen was vastly popular,
And prayed that their child might some day be
As good and as kind a Queen as she.

On their kingdom's coast, in a lonely tower
Blackened by time and rent by blast,
A Fairy of prodigious power
Had dwelt, 't was said, for ages past.

7

And, lo! upon the sands hard by
She sits and mutters moodily,
Crouching beneath her pall-like cloak,
  Nursing her crutch as she does her hate,
While the carrion crows around her croak,
  And wonder how long they have still to wait.
Up on a sudden she starts, and shrieks,
" My broom directly round to the door!"
Just as to-day Lady Ballarat speaks
  To " Buttons" who trembles her wig before!
In a minute she's mounted and scudding away
  Over hill, over dale, over lake, over bay,
Over town, over tower, over marsh, over wood,
  On that very ill wind which blows nobody good.

With flambeau and with girandole
  The palace is ablaze!
King, Queen, and every courtly soul
  Await the seven Fays,
All whose addresses they could find
Invited, as time out of mind

The custom 'twas in Fairyland,
Godmothers to the babe to stand;

Which meant, of course, that each should stand some-
Thing or other very handsome.
E'en in our day some such reflection
May guide sponsorial selection.

9

They come! They come! Their golden cars
    Make the spangled sky more bright,
And they shoot to earth like falling stars
    On a cloudless autumn night!
Ere porter, page, or chamberlain can pass the welcome word,
The seven Fairy guests are seated at the festal board.
But, ah! on that fair picture falls full soon a fearful blot—
The dark malicious features of the *eighth*, who had been forgot!

    It just occurs to me, indeed,
    Ere with my story I proceed,
    That I, perhaps, in order strict
    The royal parents should depict.

The Queen was young, and tall, and fair,
    With eyes a painter loves to study;
And had the fashionable hair,
    Between the flaxen and the ruddy.
You might have travelled far to seek,
    As any courtier would have betted,
A silkier peach-blossom cheek,
    To Rachel not the least indebted.

The King was past the middle age,
And not particularly sage;

Corpulent, careless, jovial, fond
　　Of—innocently, mind—gallanting;
He never went a step beyond.
　　　　Ate, drank, and slept—'twas whispered, snored
　　　　Right royally, and would have roared
　　　If any one had hinted—Banting!

The Banquet.

Here at the banquet him behold,
  With Fairy after Fairy flirting,
Pledging them in his cup of gold—
"A loving cup" he seems asserting;
Not being in the least aware
That o'er him by the slenderest hair
Is hanging what the poets please
To call the sword of Damocles.
Alas! over how many easy chairs
Are dangling such daggers by similar hairs!

The banquet is over; the baby brought,
And the gifts of the godmothers humbly besought.
By six they are kindly and promptly bestowed,
In the good old-fashioned Fairy mode—
Virtue and Beauty, Good-nature and Grace,
  Talent—and Taste, which is rarer to find.
The seventh has quietly quitted her place,
  And listens, unnoticed, the hangings behind.
Before they have missed her, or any word more said,
Out hobbles the spiteful old Fairy aforesaid:

12

" My young sisters have all been so liberal, King,
   They have left an old body no blessing to bring ;

And therefore, although from the deed I 'm averse,
   I 'll breathe on the sweet little darling—a curse !
     A spindle she through her hand shall run,
     And die before she be twenty-one !"

13

Up started the Queen, with a shriek that might
Have melted a heart of malachite!
The King fell back in his chair of state,
With a groan so loud, and a shock so great,
That, but for the loyal arms around,
He had brought his throne and himself to the ground;
An accident, I regret to say,
Which has happened to kings in our day.
Five Maidens of Honour fell into fits,
Two Lords in Waiting lost their wits,
Though some to credit the fact refuse,
Asserting their lordships had none to lose.

The Halberdiers ceased standing at ease,
Getting very uneasy about the knees;
Of the Gardes-du-corps, the helmed chief
Gave way perforce to his manly grief,
And to hide his tears from his steel-clad bands,
A vizor made of his clasped hands;
The Jester to jest made a vain endeavour,
And stood looking more like a fool than ever.

Just at that critical moment out skipped
The seventh Fairy, and sweetly smiled,

As up to the cradle she lightly tripped,
And touched with her wand the sleeping child.
"Dread not," she cried, "the doom you've heard:
The last is still the strongest word,

15

And that word to speak have I.
Of her wound she shall not die,
But under my protection lie
In slumber for a century;
When a charming Prince shall wake her,
And his wife with transport make her."

How could any words express
  The gratitude of Queen and King?
Yet, if the truth I must confess,
  Gratitude is so rare a thing,
Either upon or off a .throne,
That 't is in words, and words alone,
Most people's gratitude *is* shown.
Well, in this case there was nought they could do,
But *say* they were grateful, most grateful; and who,
Considering all things, can doubt it was true?

None, surely, who see that Sovereign stand
At his palace gate, with his royal hand
As nearly as possible pressed on that part
Of his portly person which covers his heart;

Or the joy that beams o'er the whole expanse
Of his Majesty's ample countenance,
As he does the best that he can to bend
And bow farewell to his Fairy friend.

And that old hag who, out of spite,
Caused by an unintended slight,
Had doomed an innocent to death,
With one cold blast of her blighting breath :
Look how she glares with impotent wrath,
  As home she drives in her dragon car,
Scaring the urchins out of her path,
  Who consider her equipage singular.
On her broom she swept to revenge with pleasure,
But returns in her sulky now at leisure.

Those of our curious readers who
Peep into old books as well as new,
May have learned that after this event
There was passed an Act of Parliament

Which made it felony to spin
With spindles, or keep spindles in
Any dwelling of any sort;
And according to the last report,
In Fairyland 't is remembered still
As the "Mustn't Spin with Spindles Bill."

Well, seventeen years have swiftly flown;
The babe has into girlhood grown,
A girlhood such as might have been,
That of the famed Egyptian Queen,
Whose love to win, the Roman cost
A world, and counted it well lost;
Or hers of Troy, whose fatal charms
For ten long years kept Greece in arms.
I leave the reader to decide,
As he may fancy, dark or fair;
Never would I presume to guide
Another's taste in matters where
" *De gustibus,*" he might protest
Clearly, " *Non disputandum est.*"

Whate'er, dear Sir, you most adore,
Fancy her that—and something more!

One fatal morning, left alone,
 And having nought on earth to do—
A state of things which oft is known
 To lead all sorts of mischief to—
Rambling the great old building round,
 In which for safety's sake they kept her,
She heard what seemed the faintest sound
  Of singing in some distant chamber ;
  And up a narrow turret stair,
 There being none to intercept her,
Through a dark low-browed porch, that frowned
  As though it bade her to beware,
 She hastily began to clamber.
Breathless, at length she stood before
An old worm-eaten oaken door,
Which on its creaking hinges swung
 Slowly and heavily to and fro,
And bore to the song behind it sung
 A burden that boded deeper woe—

'T was a sad and solemnly chanted strain,
The piteous wail of a soul in pain.

SONG.

Time was these rayless orbs were bright,
And lovers languished in their light ;
And these dull ears drank deeply in
The words that trusting maidens win.
Oh, would that Fate had been more kind,
And I been born both deaf and blind !
I had not then been left forlorn,
To wish that I had *ne'er* been born !

Who could behold that noble face,
And link it with a soul so base ?
Who could those honeyed accents hear,
And falsehood in the pleader fear ?
Come, Death, and close the lids in sleep
Of eyes that serve me but to weep !
Call from the quiet grave for me :
I listen with my heart for thee !

The singer was a wrinkled crone,
  Whom age and grief had caused to dwindle
Till she was nought but skin and bone:
And there she sat and made her moan,
  Spinning with an old-fashioned spindle,
As in defiance of the Act,
But quite unconsciously, in fact;
For, blind, she couldn't read a word of it;
And deaf, she never could have heard of it.

Ended her song, the woman wept,
  And in her lap the spindle laid,
The while with wasted hand she swept
  The tears away that slowly strayed
Adown her cheeks—sad caves of care—
  White as her wild dishevelled hair.

The Princess, who had never seen
  Such spinning in her life before,
And kept in ignorance had been
  Of the strange fate for her in store,

Lightly the threshold crossed, and bent
  Upon the work a curious eye,
Then raised the spindle with intent
  Her skill at twirling it to try.

The hour had come! At Fate's command,
The sharp point pierced the maiden's hand!
With pain till then quite unacquainted,
First she screamed, and then she fainted.

That instant through the castle rang
  Fiendish laughter, and a peal
Of thunder, followed with a clang
  That made the ancient turrets reel.
The King and Queen, and all the Court,
  Who'd just arrived upon a visit,
Hearing the terrible report,
  Had barely time to ask "What is it:'
When a strange stupor seized on all
In chamber, garden, kitchen, hall:

And to her couch by fairy aid,
  Borne like a blossom on the air,
The lovely maid was gently laid,
  A hundred years to slumber there

PART II.

COME and gone a hundred years!
  Oh, what an age it is to *say!*
Ye who have lived so long — appears
  It to ye now more than a day?
O Time! thou shouldst be counted by
  Not weeks and months, but joys and fears:
Seasons I 've known like seconds fly!
  An hour has seemed a hundred years!

A hundred Winters have shed their snows,
　To be smiled away by as many Springs;
As many Summers renewed the rose,
　And once again brown Autumn brings
His purple clusters, his yellow sheaves,
And is changing to gold the linden's leaves.
Once again the hunter's horn
Is heard on the hills at early morn,
And *through the coppice lightly bounds*
　The stag uproused from his ferny bed
By the nearer cry of the cruel hounds,
　Haughtily tossing his antlered head.
Over the plain like the wind he sweeps,
Into the river broad he leaps;
Bravely breasts the rapid tide;
Rushes up the sedgy side;
Shakes from his flanks a silver flood,
And is lost in the depths of a pathless wood.

Across the plain, and through the stream,
　Hound and huntsman have followed fast;

Over their heads the wild
  fowl scream,
And the falcon into the
  air is cast.
The heron a speedy prey
  may fall,
But the panting hounds
  are baffled all;

The hunter's knife in its sheath may stay,—
That stag will never be brought to bay.

Foremost of the cavalcade,
Halting beneath the forest shade,
Patting the neck of his noble roan,
Stood the heir to a foreign throne.
A royal youth of matchless mien,
Like the princely Dane of old,
Of fashion the glass, and of form the mould.
His riding suit of velvet green
Richly guarded with Venice gold;
Through the slashes, violet silk
Of Lyons, drawn with taste and care;
His supple boots, I trow, they were
Of cordovan of the same hue;
His cap of velvet, violet too,
From which a feather, white as milk,
Drooped gracefully. his ear behind,
Or dallied with the wooing wind.
Over his shoulder loosely flung,
A broad embroidered baldrick hung;

With tasselled horn and *gipeciere;*
A hunting-knife upon his thigh,
The hilt of sculptured ivory,
On which, 'twixt boar and man, the strife
Was carven to the very life.
  In short, I may say, without fear,
That, take his Highness altogether,
Face, figure, dress from spur to feather,
    A more bewitching cavalier
Ne'er stepped in shoe- or in boot-leather.

Hither he sailed in quest of sport,
But never a King and never a Court
Has he heard of since he leapt ashore,
And he wonders who rules this island o'er.
Nothing with life, save beast or bird,
    Has hitherto met his eager eye;
No rustic tending flock or herd,
    No traveller plodding the footpath by;
No maiden at a cottage door,
Teaching the woodbine to clamber o'er;

No cottage!—and therefore there couldn't be
A maiden at its door to see.
There reigns a silence, solemn and strange,
  Unbroken, save by the bittern's cry,
Or the whimper of the dogs that range
  Around the forest hopelessly:
The staunchest hound in all the pack
Has slunk with a howl from the brushwood back;
The hardiest hunter in all the train
Has striven to enter that wood in vain.
The stag, they swear, must a fairy have been,
To have passed those serried trunks between!
—They were not so much out, as will soon be seen.

The Prince, who has mounted a hillock, sees,
Over the tops of the tallest trees,
A castle in the distance rear
  Its battlements grey on a rocky steep,
Fenced around by that forest drear:
  The flanking towers and massive heep
*Of venerable age appear,** *

               * *Vide* heading to Part II.

And suddenly to his mind recalls
  Of his Breton nurse a ballad old,
And wonders whether those wood-girt walls
  The charm of his boyish dreams enfold.
The fancy moves him more and more
As he murmurs the ancient legend o'er,
To the melody quaint of that simple rhyme
Which his cradle has rocked to many a time
Long before he the words could scan,
And hope in his heart he might be the man !

BALLAD.

In a wood there is a tower,
       Sing a-down, a-down-a !
In the tower a lady's bower,
       Sing a-down, a-down-a !
In the bower a maiden fair,
       Sing a-down, a-down-a !
Day and night she slumbers there,
       Sing a-down, a-down-a !

31

None may thread that forest deep,
None ascend that castle keep,
None may break that maiden's sleep,
   Sing a-down, a-down-a!

Where the wood, I pray ye, show,
   Sing a-down, a-down-a!
Through which Cupid cannot go?
   Sing a-down, a-down-a!
Where the castle walled about,
   Sing a-down, a-down-a!
Strong enough to keep him out?
   Sing a-down, a-down-a!
Love the destined Prince shall guide
To the Sleeping Beauty's side,
With a kiss to wake his bride!
   Sing a-down, a-down-a!

There are twenty verses more or so;
But two are enough, I trow, to show
The sort of stuff they sang long ago
To an infant heir to a crown-a!
And which now would never go "down-a."

The Prince, however, paused not then
   Or words or tune to criticise;
But shouted to his merry men—
     Not that his men were really merry—
   In fact they were quite otherwise—
     Sulky at being thrown out, very;
But so 'twas the fashion them to call,
And therefore he shouted, "My merry men all!
We have lost a stag; but what if here
In this covert is lodged a dainty *dear?*
'Tis a *hind* that my *heart* is fain to follow,
If the wood will give me a fair view-*hollow!*"

Shockingly bad, I must confess;
But then in the days of Good Queen Bess,
     That golden age
     Of the English stage,
Such plays upon words were quite the rage.
Then why should critics vent their ire on
The puns of Brough, Burnand, and Byron?
They only do, with more decorum,
What the Swan of Avon did before 'em.

The merry men had not a guess
  Of what his Royal Highness meant;
But so harangued, could do no less
  Than give him full and free consent
To follow his own inclinations;
As persons in exalted stations
Will sometimes do without permission :
  And so they filled him a stirrup cup,
And drinking success to his expedition,
  With loud hurrahs they cheered him up.

The spur he gave to his noble horse;
O'er crimson heath and golden gorse
Galloped the steed at a *pas de charge*,
Nor swerved when he came to the thorny marge
Of the dark, dense wood, but cleared at a bound
  The triple, tall *cheval de frise*
Of brambles fencing it all around,
  And dashed at the nearest rank of trees,
As he would have done, at the trumpet's sound,
  'Gainst a troop of hostile cavalry.

Wonder! oh, wonder!
They move asunder,
　And leave to the Prince an entrance free!
As on he presses the wood divides,
And up the steep ascent he rides,
With flushing cheek and beating heart;
Not seeing who plays an opening part
In this fairy "*Piece de circonstance*,"
And yet did he upwards cast a glance,
He might mark where, in the clear blue sky,

All light and white as a fleecy cloud,
A female form floats gracefully ;
At whose fairy fingers' slightest touch,
Their branches tangled never so much,
The gnarled oaks relax their clutch,

And towering pines, and cedars proud,
Limes, and elms, and beeches bow
Their lofty heads in homage low,
And backward at her bidding go
On either hand. The forest through
Forming a stately avenue
The very gates of the castle to.

The drawbridge is down — the castle doors
  All open: he hastes from his steed to leap.

Stretched on a settle the warder snores,
Leaving his wicket itself to keep.
  He enters the courtyard. *'Gainst the wall*
An aged falconer, hawk on hand,
And a gay young courtier lounging stand,

Apparently in earnest talk.
In the mystery of hawking deep
    They might have been; but falconer, hawk,
    And gay gallant are each and all
At present very fast asleep.
Into the guard-room he passes. Lo!
The yeomen are sleeping all in a row;

Good men and true — deny it who will —
Under arms they are standing still.

Into the cellar, a passing peep
Shows him *the butler fallen asleep*
Over a hogshead of Malvoisie —
Flagon and cup both empty be.

Look at his nose,
You can well suppose
He had helped himself to whichever was stronger,
Till the drowsy spell
Upon him fell,
And he couldn't help himself any longer.

In the banquet-hall, *around*
The great oak table, some eight or ten
Noble lords and gentlemen
Of the privy council next he found

Seated all in slumber sound,
  Nodding over their fruit and wine,
Just as they might have slept and snored
O'er matters of weight at the council-board.
  They had clearly been lucky enough to dine
Before the fate they could not avert
  For the first time made them, I opine,
Unconscious of their own desert.

He mounts a flight of marble stairs,
  And in an anteroom discovers
  A maid of honour taking a nap,
  And near her one of a score of lovers.
She had been reading — what? Her prayers?
  The book lay open in her lap —
It might be a missal, and it might not —
It matters little at this time what —
There are so many books, both great and small,
O'er which one is certain asleep to fall,
That a charm is more needed now to make
The reader of them keep awake.

But 'tis plain enough that the saucy youth
Was about to snatch a kiss, forsooth!

She wasn't asleep *then*, I suspect;
For a close observer may detect

Her hand is raised to wave him away —
Though a smile on her cheek remains, to say
She wouldn't frown if he didn't obey.

Into the presence-chamber, there
The King reclines in his great arm-chair;
  The Queen on his shoulder calmly reposes;
Her parrot near her has found a perch,
And is like their Majesties, "fast as a church."
 The court fool, crouched at his master's foot,
   In his motley suit —
   As his bauble mute —
Dreams of how many his cap might wear
 If placed on the heads of all it fits.
  Behind him a page on the chair-back dozes;
And proudly in front of the royal pair,
 The Queen's pet pug in a dog's sleep sits,
  Upturning the pertest of all pug noses.
   To the ground has rolled
   A cup of gold,
Dropped by the King in his sore dismay,
 When they suddenly filled his cup of woe

With the news of his daughter's fate that day,
Exactly one hundred years ago!

But where is she — that matchless fair
A fated Prince shall win and wear,
The Beauty born. to be *his* bride?
    For, oh! no longer can he doubt

For whom the matted boughs divide —
For whom the portals open wide.
  Yet when was love its fears without?
So often when its hopes are highest —
So often when the goal is nighest —
Beguiled, betrayed, deserted, crost —
The deepest, truest, tried the most!
His heart, but now that wildly beat,
  Has almost ceased a pulse to know;
His breath he holds — his eager feet
  Seem suddenly to earth to grow.

At the end of a corridor,
A closely curtained porch before,
  He stands transfixed, as though he were
Only one human being more
Subjected to the fairy spell,
  And for a century had there
Remained a sleeping sentinel.

Fate will not suffer longer pause.
Aside, with trembling hand, he draws

The drapery of cloth of gold,
That falls in many a gorgeous fold
From the rich cornice to the floor,
And gently touches the gilded door
That open in an instant flies,
Disclosing to his dazzled eyes
  A chamber filled with rosy light,
    Which from some fount mysterious flings
Its tender rays upon a bed
Of silver tissue, canopied
  With velvet as the snow-drift white,
Looped up with bands of orient pearl,
  And curtained round with lace so fine,
    The gossamer might claim the work.
  Fairies and elves in mazy rings
Throughout it seem to dance and whirl,
    Or in the filmy meshes lurk,
  As guardians of the form divine;
Fit jewel for a case so rare,
In charmed sleep recumbent there.

O happy Prince, whom love and fate
  To favour have their powers allied!
By fate impelled — with love elate —
  One bound has brought him to her side!
There is a whirring in his ears
  As of a thousand tiny wings,
And animated now appears
  Each elf and fay in all the rings
Wrought in those curtains fine and rare,
Which melt, at his approach, to air;
      And o'er his head, and round the bed,
      By the protecting Fairy led,
      Group after group revolving fly
      In joyous wild expectancy! *

He sees or heeds them not: for one
Sole object hath he sight alone.
He lifts the long luxuriant tresses
  That partly veil her cheek — he takes
Her hand — his lips on hers he presses.—
  The spell is o'er — she starts, she wakes

* *Vide* Frontispiece.

48

Raises to him in sweet surprise
Her large and lustrous loving eyes.
" And is it you, my Prince?"——Oh, why
Record his rapturous reply?
Indeed, who is there at this day
Knows what the Prince did really say?
E'en the first teller of the tale
Felt there his information fail;
And can I, then, expected be
To know it, any more than he?
Besides, the author always flings
  On you the burthen and the bother,
To fancy all the charming things
  The lovers said to one another.
Moreover, by his computation,
They talked four hours without cessation! *
And why the breaking of the spell,
And all that there and then befell,
Should I in random rhyme rehearse,
  When England's laurelled bard hath sung,

---

* " *Enfin il y avoit quartres heures quil's se parloient.*"
LA BELLE AU BOIS DORMANTE.

With all the power of English verse
  And all the charm of English tongue,
The rushing back to love or strife
Of " all that long-pent stream of life ":
What folly to attempt to rival,
Of that sweet " Day-dream," " The Revival." *

No; here my task I gladly close:
  No more the pencil claims the pen;
And every child the story knows,
  And all that happened " after then."
Rather, as free the Laureate leaves
  Each one, according to his mind
Or any web his fancy weaves,
  A meaning to the tale to find,
Let me conclude with a translation
Of Charles Perrault's own *pero*-ration.

* Poems by Alfred Tennyson, Poet Laureate. 12mo.
London: Moxon, 1855.

L'Envoy.

"Some time for a husband to wait,
   Who is young, handsome, wealthy, and tender,
May not be a hardship too great
   For a maid whom love happy would render;
But to be for a century bound
   To live single, I fancy the number
Of Beauties but small would be found
   So long who would patiently slumber.
To lovers who hate time to waste,
   And minutes as centuries measure,
I would hint, those who marry in haste,
   May live to repent it at leisure;
Yet so ardently onward they press,
   And on prudence so gallantly trample,
That I haven't the heart, I confess,
   To urge on them Beauty's example." *

* Four and Twenty Fairy Tales. By Perrault and others. 12mo.
London: G. Routledge and Co., 1858.

51

DALZIEL BROTHERS
Camden Press
ENGRAVERS & PRINTERS

DALZIELS' FINE ART GIFT BOOK FOR 1866.

ONE GUINEA.

In a Superb Binding, richly Illuminated in Red, Blue, and Gold, 4to.,

A ROUND OF DAYS

DESCRIBED IN

ORIGINAL POEMS

BY SOME OF

OUR MOST CELEBRATED POETS,

AND IN

PICTURES

BY

EMINENT ARTISTS,

ENGRAVED BY THE BROTHERS DALZIEL.

List of Contributors.

AUTHORS.

WILLIAM ALLINGHAM	MARY HOWITT
ROBERT BUCHANAN	JENNETT HUMPHREYS
DR. DULCKEN	JEAN INGELOW
AMELIA B. EDWARDS	FREDERICK LOCKER
DORA GREENWELL	GEORGE MACDONALD
TOM HOOD	THE HON. MRS. NORTON
WILLIAM HOWITT	CHRISTINA G. ROSSETTI

TOM TAYLOR
THE AUTHOR OF "THE GENTLE LIFE"
AND THE AUTHOR OF "JOHN HALIFAX, GENTLEMAN."

ARTISTS.

W. P. BURTON	T. DALZIEL	J. W. NORTH
A. W. BAYES	PAUL GRAY	G. J. PINWELL
WARWICK BROOKS	A. B. HOUGHTON	F. WALKER
E. DALZIEL	T. MORTEN	J. D. WATSON

The work is printed throughout on a fine India paper tint, and contains

FORTY ORIGINAL POEMS and SEVENTY PICTURES.

"As life consists of 'a round of days,' that title has been chosen to designate a collection of Poems and Pictures representing every-day scenes, occurrences, and incidents in various phases of existence."

In Demy 4to., Extra Cloth, Chaste Design in Gold by JOHN LEIGHTON, F.S.A.,
One Guinea.

HOME THOUGHTS AND HOME SCENES.

IN

THIRTY-FIVE ORIGINAL POEMS

BY

| HON. MRS. NORTON | DORA GREENWELL | JEAN INGELOW |
| JENNETT HUMPHREYS | A. B. EDWARDS | MRS. TOM TAYLOR |

AND THE AUTHOR OF "JOHN HALIFAX, GENTLEMAN."

AND

THIRTY-FIVE ELABORATE PICTURES BY A. B. HOUGHTON,

ENGRAVED BY THE BROTHERS DALZIEL.

"We predict popularity, and a deserved popularity, for this production."—*Saturday Review.*

Elaborate Binding, Full Gilt, One Guinea.

THE PARABLES OF OUR LORD.

WITH PICTURES BY J. E. MILLAIS, R.A.,

ENGRAVED BY THE BROTHERS DALZIEL.

Red Lettered, and Printed on Fine Toned Paper.

"In these designs we have much of Mr. Millais' finest work, whilst Messrs. Dalziel have raised the character of wood engraving by their exact and most admirable translations."—*Reader.*

Superb Binding, Designed by OWEN JONES, *One Guinea.*

BIRKET FOSTER'S

PICTURES OF ENGLISH LANDSCAPE.

(ENGRAVED BY THE BROTHERS DALZIEL),

WITH PICTURES IN WORDS BY TOM TAYLOR.

"Here is a Birket Foster 'Gallery' of thirty pictures for a guinea. Pictures so carefully finished, that they would be graceful ornaments were they cut out of the books and framed."—*Examiner.*